Everybody Knows *That!*

Weekly Reader Children's Book Club presents

Everybody Knows *That!*

by Susan Pearson
pictures by Diane Paterson

THE DIAL PRESS | *New York*

This book is a presentation of Weekly
Reader Children's Book Club.
Weekly Reader Children's Book Club
offers book clubs for children from
preschool to young adulthood. All
quality hardcover books are selected
by a distinguished Weekly Reader
Selection Board.

For further information write to:
Weekly Reader Children's Book Club
1250 Fairwood Ave.
Columbus, Ohio 43216

Published by The Dial Press
One Dag Hammarskjold Plaza
New York, New York 10017

Text copyright © 1978 by Susan Pearson
Pictures copyright © 1978 by Diane Paterson
All rights reserved
Printed in the United States of America
Designed by Jane Byers Bierhorst

Library of Congress Cataloging
in Publication Data

Pearson, Susan.
Everybody knows *that!*

Summary: A young girl decides to teach her
playmate a lesson after he lets her know she can't
do certain things because she's a girl.
[1. Sex role—Fiction] I. Paterson, Diane,
1946–   II. Title.
PZ7.P323316Ev   [E]   78-51311
ISBN 0-8037-2417-9
ISBN 0-8037-2418-7 lib. bdg.

For Inge Bickel

Everybody Knows *That!*

Patty lived on the corner of Central Street and Auburn Avenue. Herbie lived in the middle of the block. They were best friends.

When Patty got the chicken pox, Herbie sent her a get-well card every day. And when she wasn't contagious anymore, he sat on her bed and played cards with her. When Herbie got stung by a bee, Patty told him to put mud on the sting to make it stop burning. And she promised not to tell anyone that they'd been in the bee tree.

Some days they played electric trains. Some days they baked cookies. Some days they played cops and robbers in the vacant lot. Some days they played dolls in the attic. But today they were going to do something extra special. Today Patty and Herbie were starting kindergarten.

The kindergarten room was wonderful. It was painted in different bright colors and had lots of windows with checkered curtains that were always open. And there were all sorts of trucks and a big sandbox and millions of blocks to build roads with. There were lots of other children and a nice teacher, Mrs. Brown, who played the piano and taught them songs and read stories to them.

"I'm going to like this," Patty told Herbie on Monday.

On Tuesday Patty and Herbie and Micky and Jason were playing trucks in the sandbox. They built roads through the sand with blocks. Herbie had the moving van, Jason had the tow truck, Micky had the jeep, and Patty had the dump truck.

"Patty," said Jason, "why don't you go play dolls with the other girls?"

"Because I like playing trucks today," said Patty.

"Patty has some neat trucks at home," said Herbie.

"Maybe," said Jason. "But girls should play dolls."

On Wednesday Mrs. Brown read the class a story about airplanes. Then she said, "Let's build an airplane out of blocks." When the plane was finished, Mrs. Brown put chairs inside for the passengers and three more chairs in the cockpit for the pilot and the co-pilot and the navigator.

"Who wants to be the pilot?" she asked. Herbie and Jason and Micky and Patty raised their hands.

"Herbie can be the pilot," said Mrs. Brown. "And Jason can be the co-pilot. Micky can be the navigator. And Patty, you can be the stewardess."

"I don't want to be the stewardess," said Patty.

"You can be a passenger then," said Mrs. Brown.

Thursday afternoon Patty walked up the street to Herbie's. Jason and Micky were already there. They were playing plane in the backyard with Herbie.

"*Rrrr, rrrr, rrrr,*" said Herbie. "Hey, Patty, you wanna be the stewardess?"

"No," said Patty. "I wanna be the pilot. You be the stewardess for a while."

"Boys aren't stewardesses," said Jason. "And girls aren't pilots."

"Why not?" said Patty.

"Everybody knows why not," said Jason.

"I don't," said Patty. "Do you know why not, Herbie?"

"Sure," said Herbie. "*Everybody* knows *that.*"

Patty went home.

Friday morning Patty was waiting for Herbie. Patty's house was closer to school, so every day Herbie rang the bell and they walked together. But on Friday no bell rang. Patty waited and waited. She went to the dining-room window and looked out. No Herbie.

"Maybe Herbie's sick," said Patty.

Then she saw Jason and Micky and Herbie coming down the street. Patty pulled on her sweater and went out the front door. But Herbie didn't stop. He didn't even look at Patty's house. He and Jason and Micky just walked on by.

"That Herbie is making me mad," said Patty, and she walked to school alone.

After school Herbie and Micky and Jason played plane again. Patty sat in the apple tree and watched them.

"I'm a bomber," Patty yelled down to them. "And you'd better watch out or I'll bomb your crummy plane to bits! *Rrrr.* Pow! Pow!" She threw apples down on them.

"You're not a bomber," said Herbie. "You're just a silly girl."

"Herbie," said Patty. "This is dumb. Why can't we play two planes? You can be the pilot of one, and I can be the pilot of the other, and Micky and Jason can be the co-pilots."

"Because we don't have enough people to be navigators and stewardesses for two planes," said Herbie. "If you wanna play, then you have to be the stewardess."

"Oh, phooey," said Patty. "I didn't want to play with you anyway."

On Saturday morning there was a knock at the back door. Patty answered it. It was Herbie.

"What do *you* want?" Patty asked him.

"My mom and dad went to see my grandpa in the hospital," said Herbie. "Your mom is supposed to baby-sit me."

"Oh," said Patty. "Well, we're baking cookies. You can play with my trucks if you want."

"Why should I play with your trucks?" said Herbie. "I want to bake cookies with you."

"Well, you can't bake cookies," Patty told him.

"Why not?" Herbie asked.

"Everybody knows why not," said Patty. "Only girls can bake cookies."

Mother rolled out the dough. Patty cut out gingerbread men and rabbits and chickens and stars. While the first batch was in the oven, Mother mixed up frosting in three separate bowls. One bowl had white frosting, one had yellow, and one had pink. Patty got out the raisins and the sprinkles. When the cookies were done, Mother cut out the second batch while Patty decorated the first.

"I could do that," said Herbie.

"No, you couldn't," said Patty. She painted one gingerbread boy pink. She gave him raisins for buttons and eyes and a mouth. She painted one rabbit yellow and sprinkled him with chocolate sprinkles. She licked the frosting off her fingers. Herbie sat on a stool and watched.

When the last batch of cookies was in the oven, Patty asked, "Can I lick the bowl?"

"Sure," said Mother.

"Me too?" asked Herbie.

"Oh, no," said Patty. "Only people who helped can lick the bowl."

"But you wouldn't let me help," said Herbie.

"That's all right," said Patty. "You wouldn't let me be the pilot."

"This is dumb," said Herbie.

"That's what I've been telling you," said Patty.

"What do you say we all three lick the bowl," said Mother. "Then we can all three decorate the last batch of cookies."

"That's a good idea," said Herbie. "And then we can play plane. It's your turn to be the pilot, Patty."

"Let's play courtroom instead," said Patty. "I think I'd rather be a judge."

About the Author

Susan Pearson is the author of several books for young readers, including *Izzie,* which was a *New York Times* Outstanding Book of the Year and a Child Study Association Book of the Year in 1975 and an ALA Children's Book of International Interest. Her most recent book is *That's Enough for One Day, J.P.!*

Ms. Pearson divides her time between writing and editing children's books. She grew up in Boston, Massachusetts, and St. Paul, Minnesota, and now lives in Brooklyn, New York.

About the Artist

Diane Paterson is the author-illustrator of a number of picture books, including *The Biggest Snowstorm Ever,* of which *Publishers Weekly* said, "the pictures are unusually inspired," and *Smile for Auntie,* of which *Kirkus Review Service* said, "[It] should get a smile out of almost anyone."

Ms. Paterson was born in Brooklyn, New York, and studied at the Pratt Institute. She now lives in High Falls, New York, with her two daughters.

And so Patty and Herbie decorated the cookies and licked the bowl. Then they both went to play courtroom. Patty was the judge.

Aprille Williams.